Stickmen's Science Stars

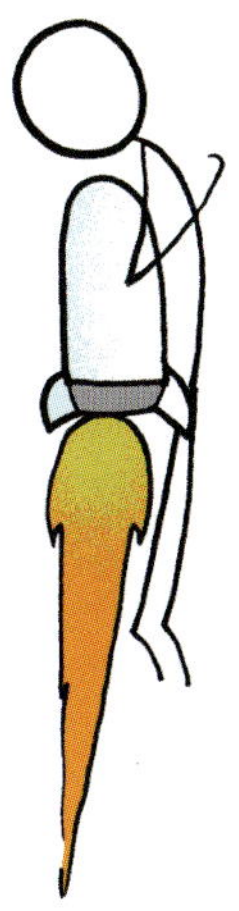

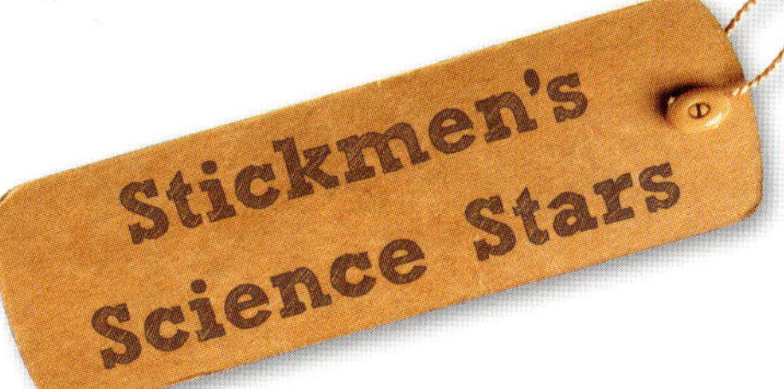

ELECTRICITY

What makes stuff work?

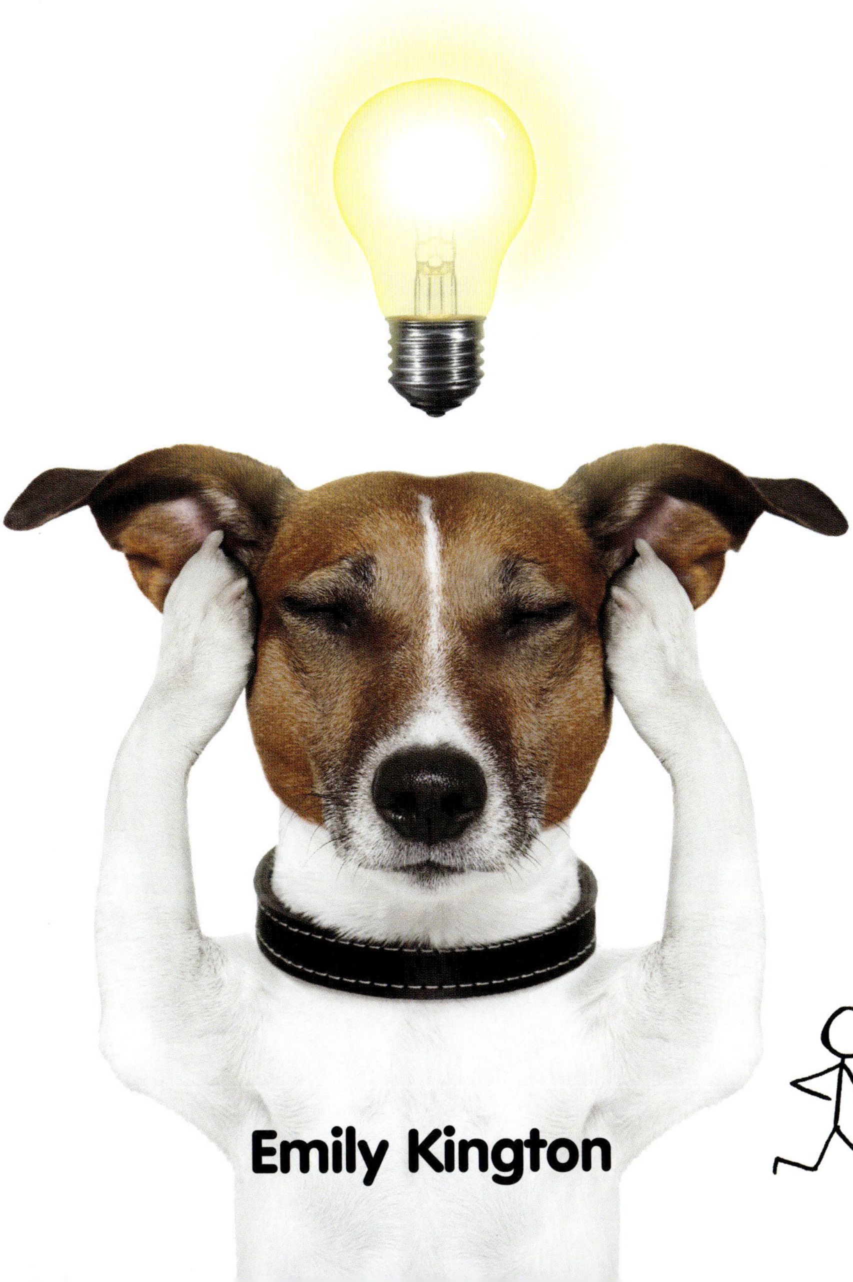

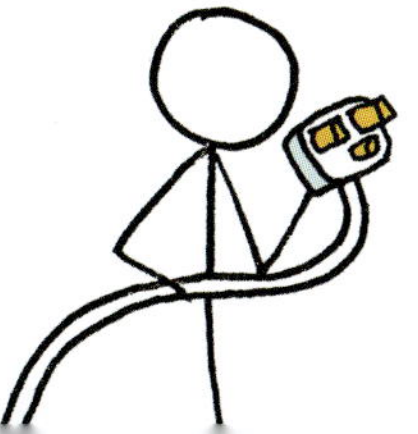

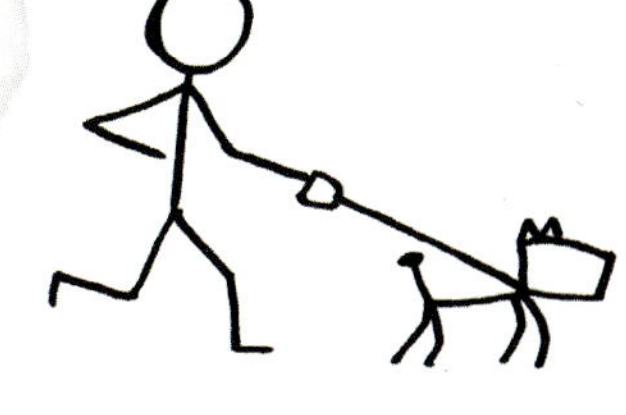

Emily Kington

Electricity keeps the lights on at night so we can see when it is dark.

CONTENTS

Words that appear in **bold** are explained in the glossary. The answers to the questions are on pages 20–21.

www.hungrytomato.com

WHAT IS ELECTRICITY?

Electricity is a kind of energy that we use in many different ways.

Electricity is used to make heat and **light**. Many houses have electric heating and lighting.

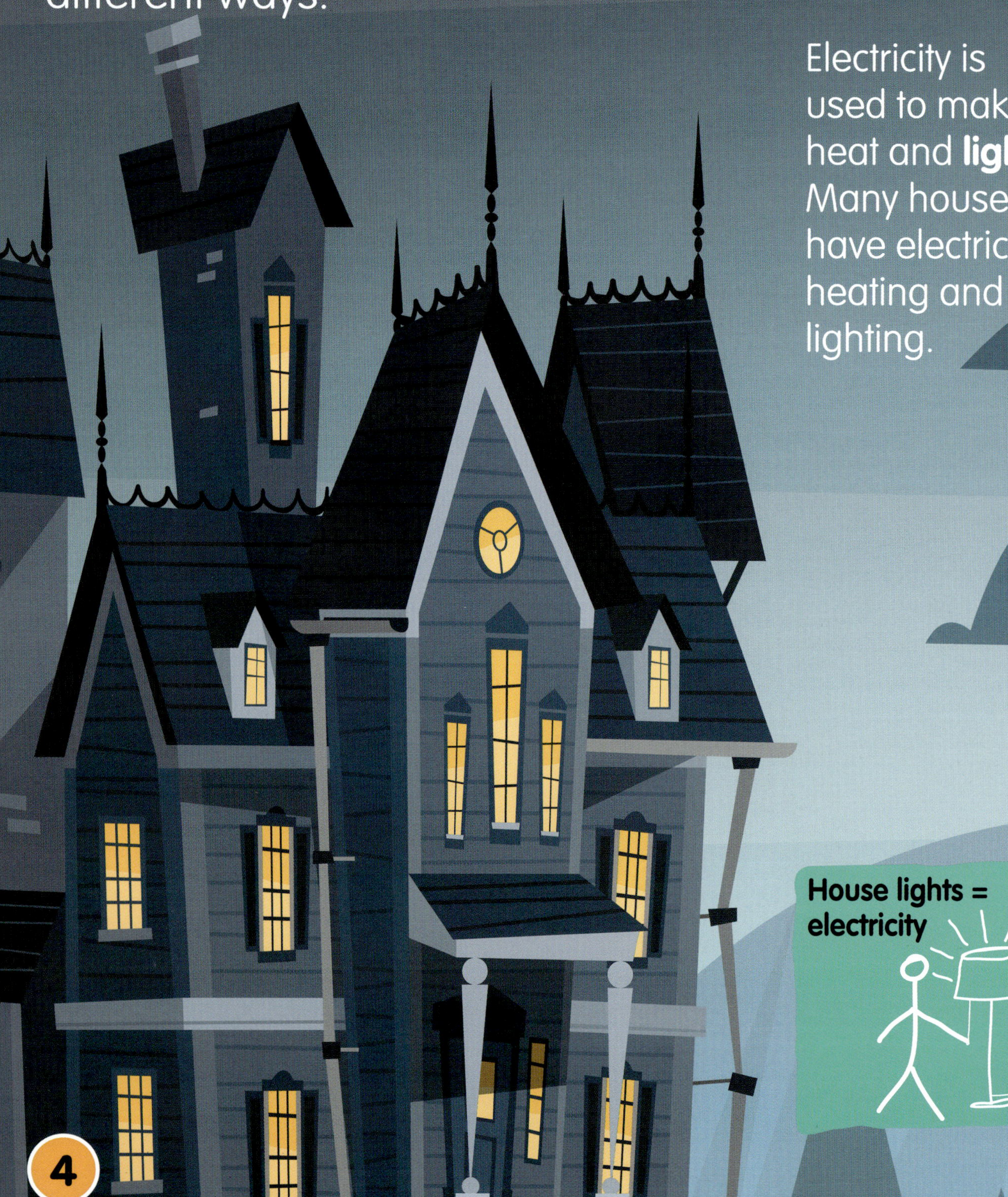

Stickmen's Challenge Now it's your turn . . .

Flashlight

When you turn on a flashlight it makes light. What kind of energy do you think a flashlight uses to make light?

Electricity makes lots of different machines work. Televisions, cell phones and computers all use electricity.

LIGHT BULBS

An electrical **light bulb** is a hollow, glass object that produces light.

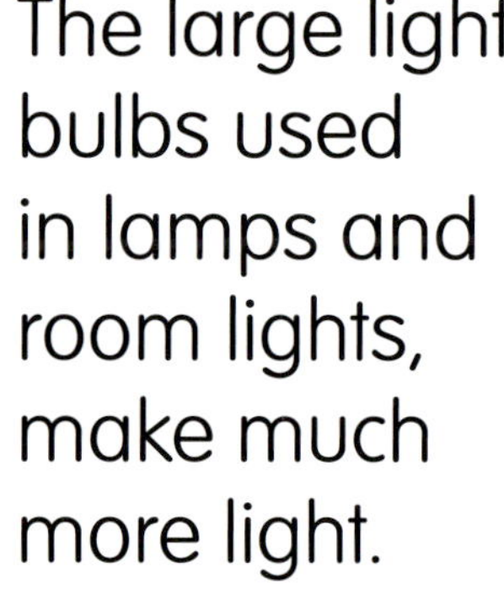

The large light bulbs used in lamps and room lights, make much more light.

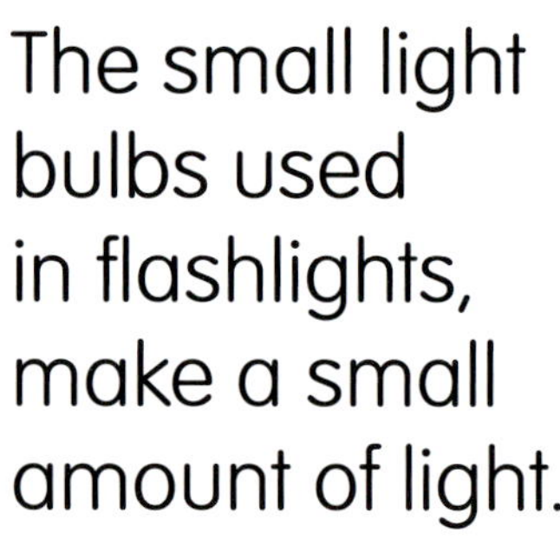

The small light bulbs used in flashlights, make a small amount of light.

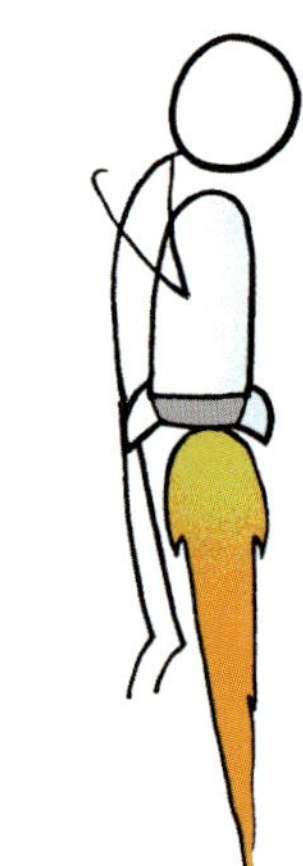

A light bulb + electricity = light

When electricity goes through the wire it makes the wire very hot. The wire gets so hot that it glows brightly.

Inside a light bulb is a thin, **metal** wire.

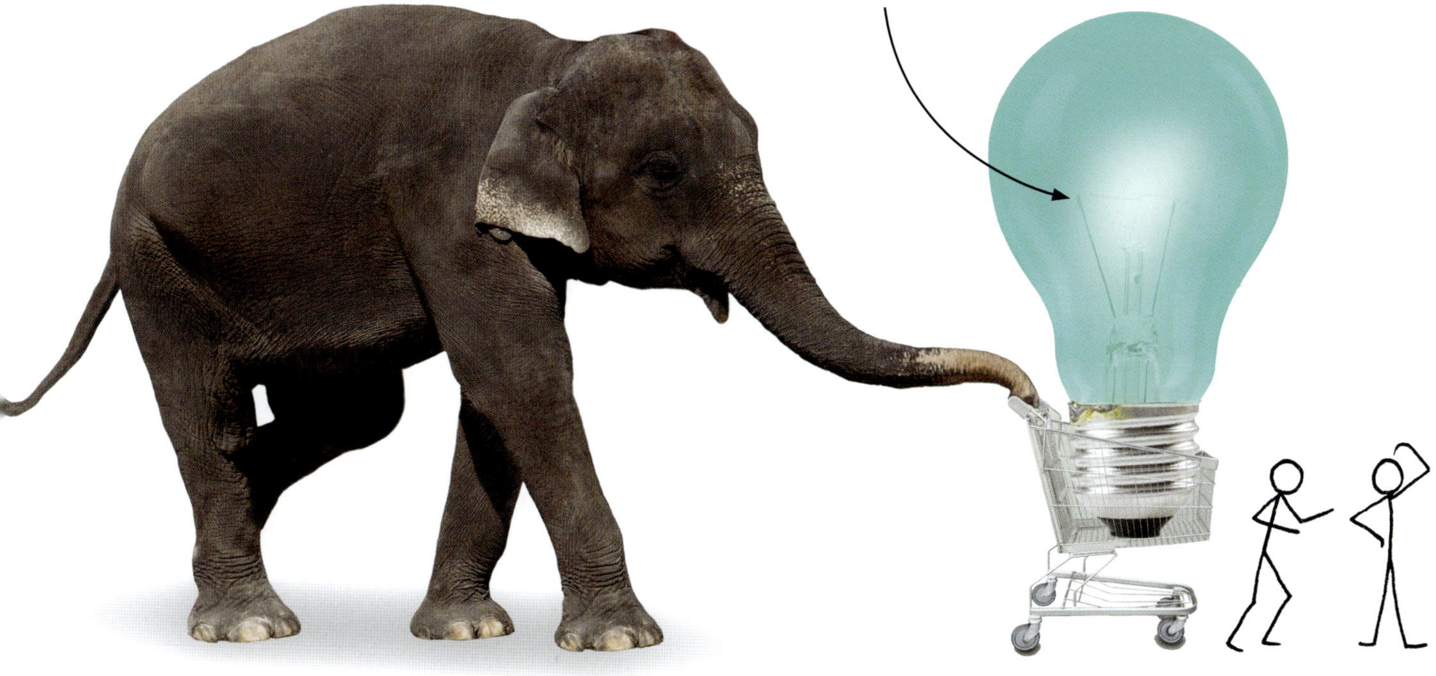

Stickmen's Challenge Now it's your turn . . .

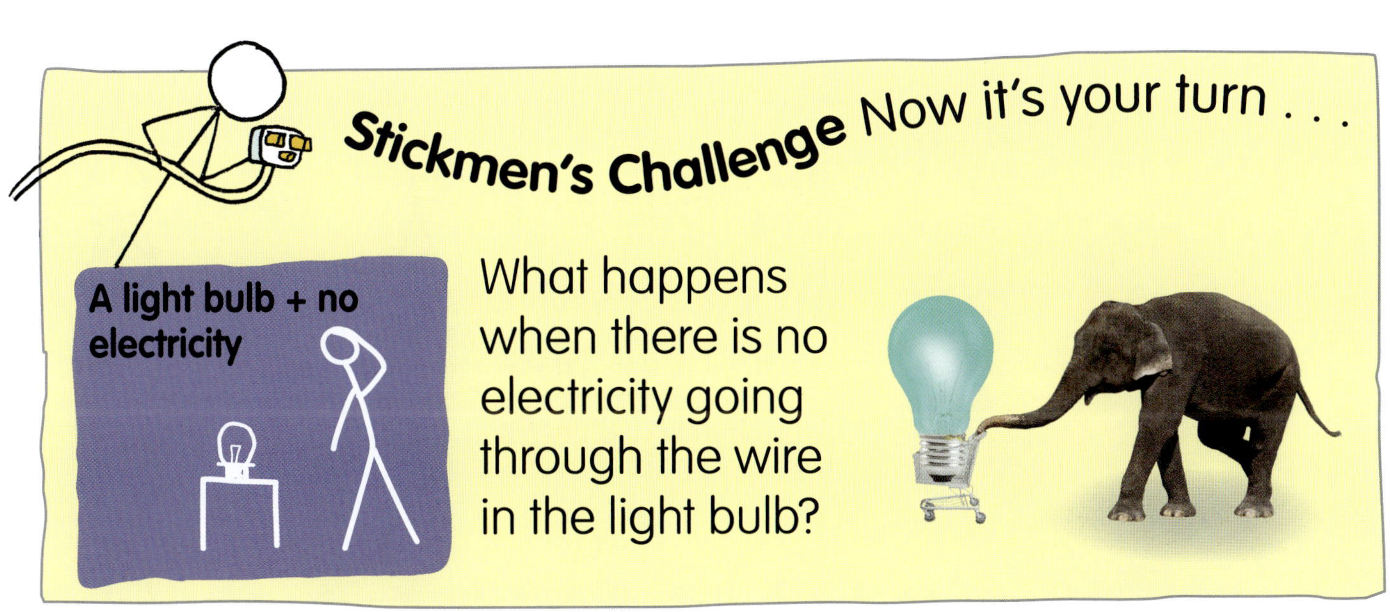

What happens when there is no electricity going through the wire in the light bulb?

BATTERIES

Batteries are a safe way to store small amounts of electricity. Every battery has two areas of bare metal. These are usually at the ends of the battery.

A battery has to be put in the right way or the flashlight will not work.

The metal ends are marked with the symbols "+" and "–".

To put the battery in, match the "+" on the battery with the "+" on the flashlight.

Do you think both flashlight A and flashlight B will work?

CIRCUITS

An electrical **circuit** is a nonstop pathway that electricity can flow through.

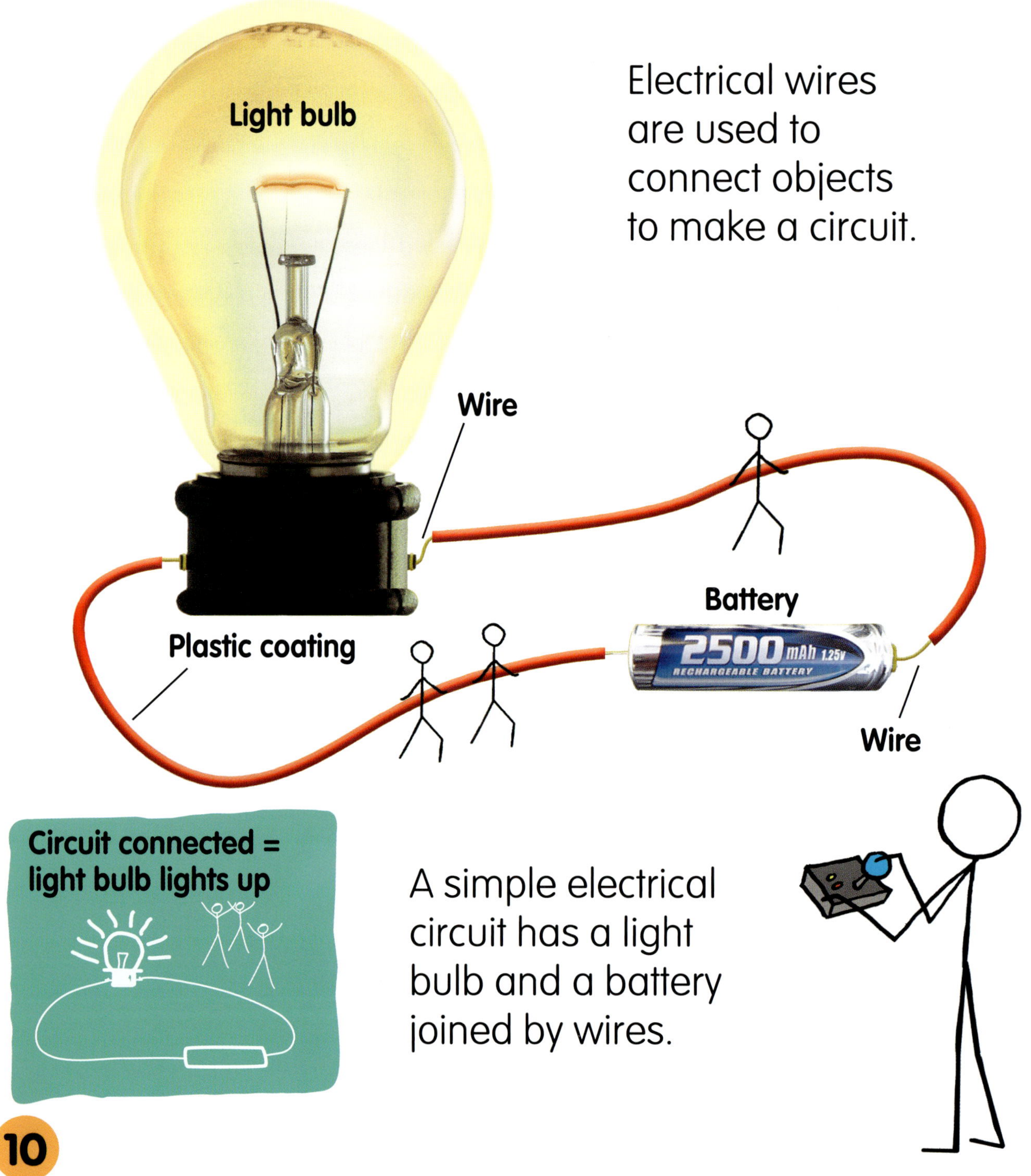

Electrical wires are used to connect objects to make a circuit.

A simple electrical circuit has a light bulb and a battery joined by wires.

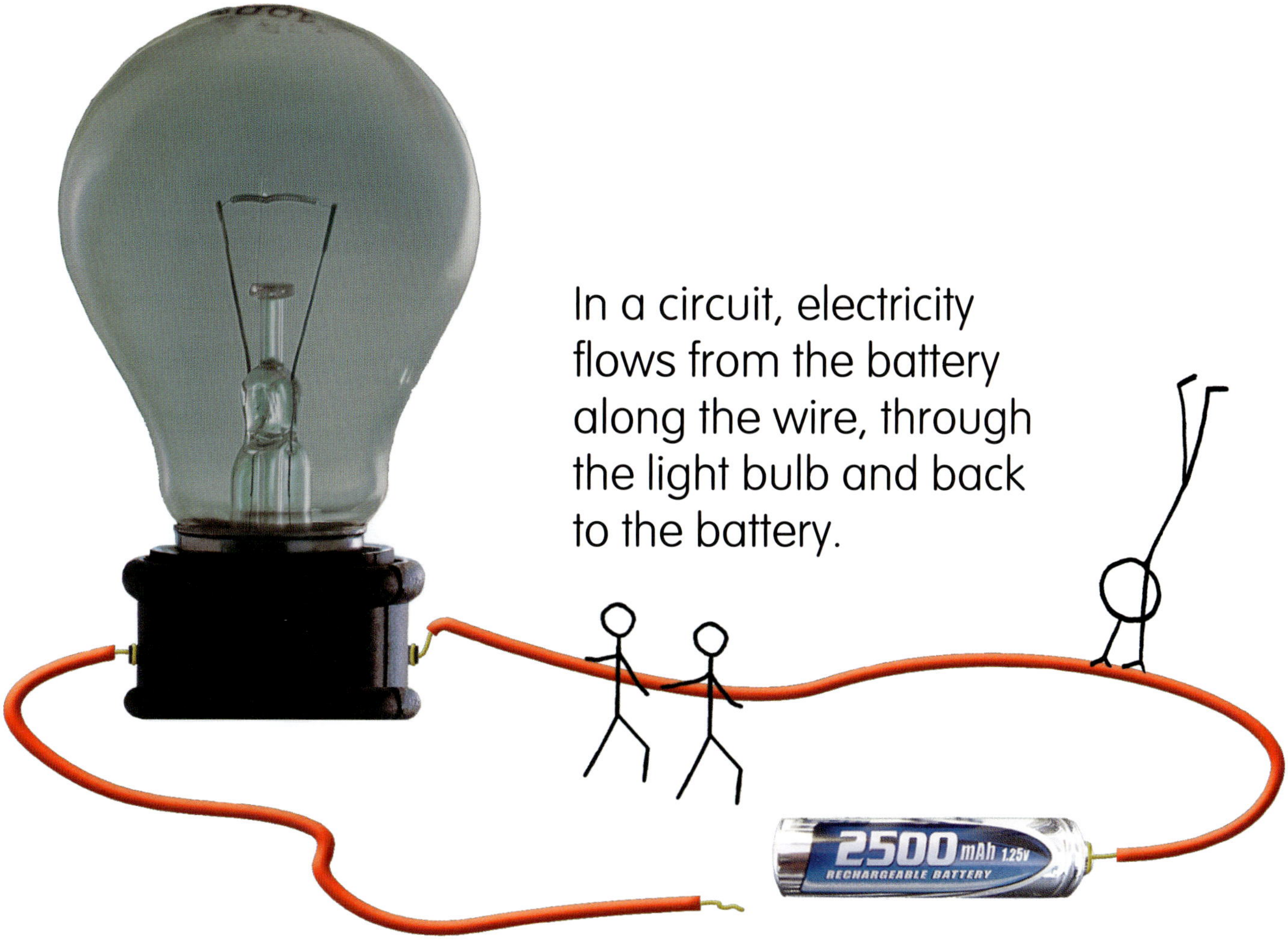

In a circuit, electricity flows from the battery along the wire, through the light bulb and back to the battery.

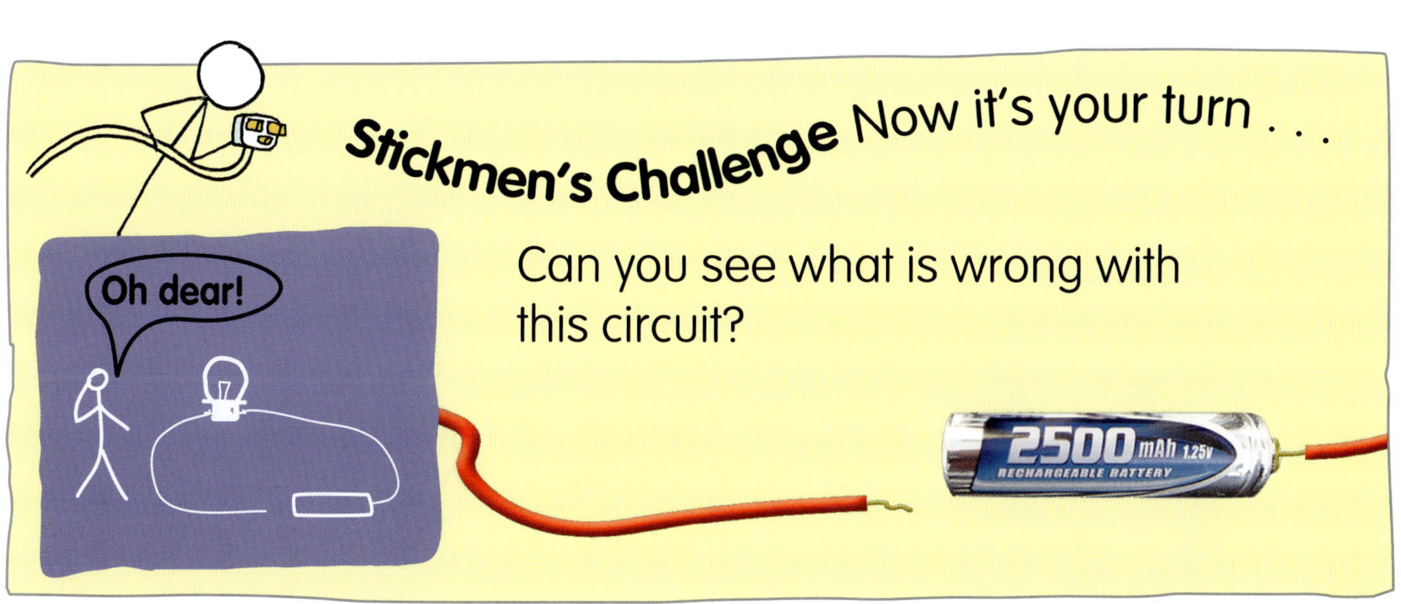

Stickmen's Challenge Now it's your turn . . .

Can you see what is wrong with this circuit?

SWITCHES

An electrical **switch** is used to control the flow of electricity around a circuit.

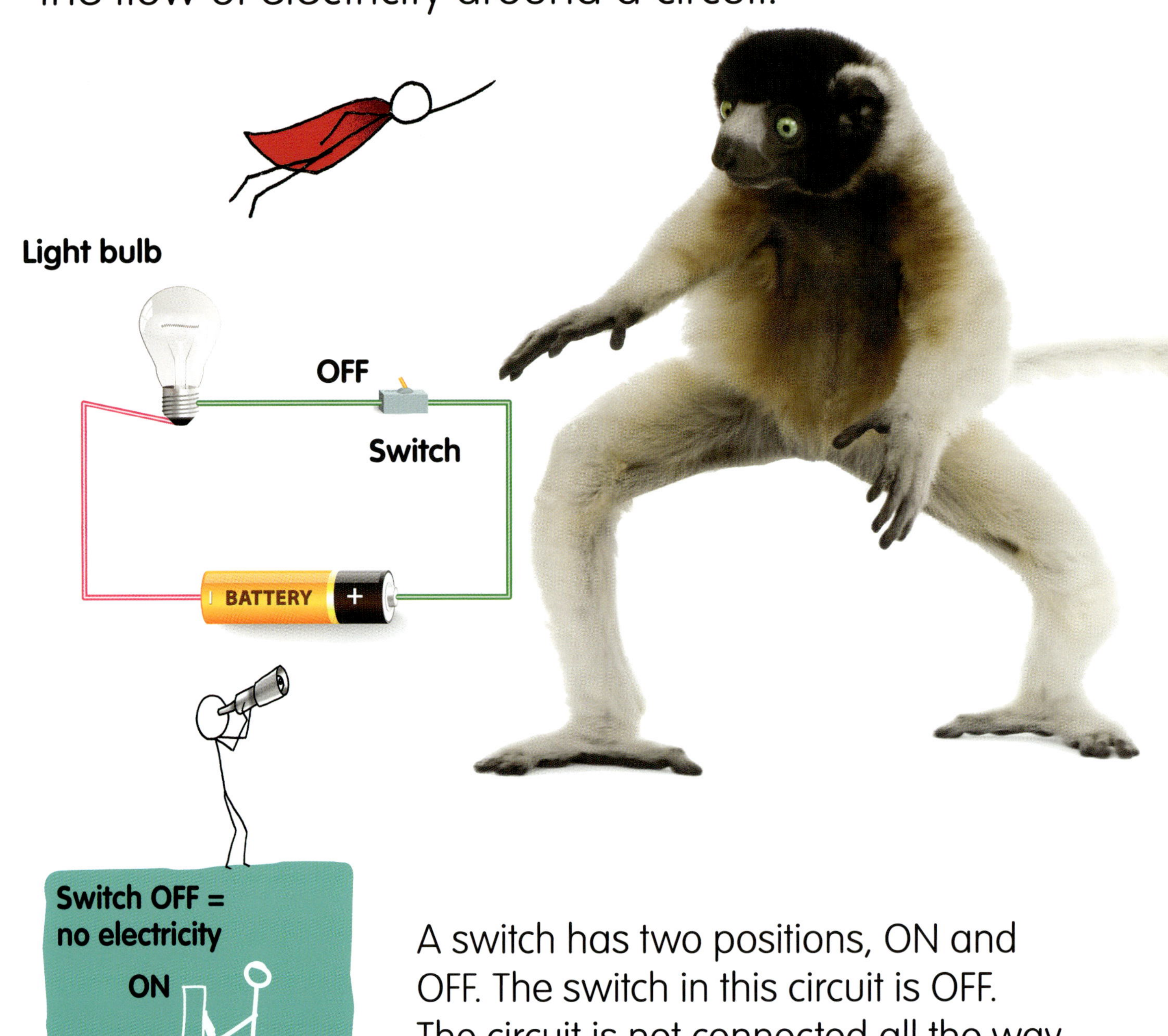

A switch has two positions, ON and OFF. The switch in this circuit is OFF. The circuit is not connected all the way around, so the electricity cannot flow.

A firebug doesn't need a battery as it makes it own light.

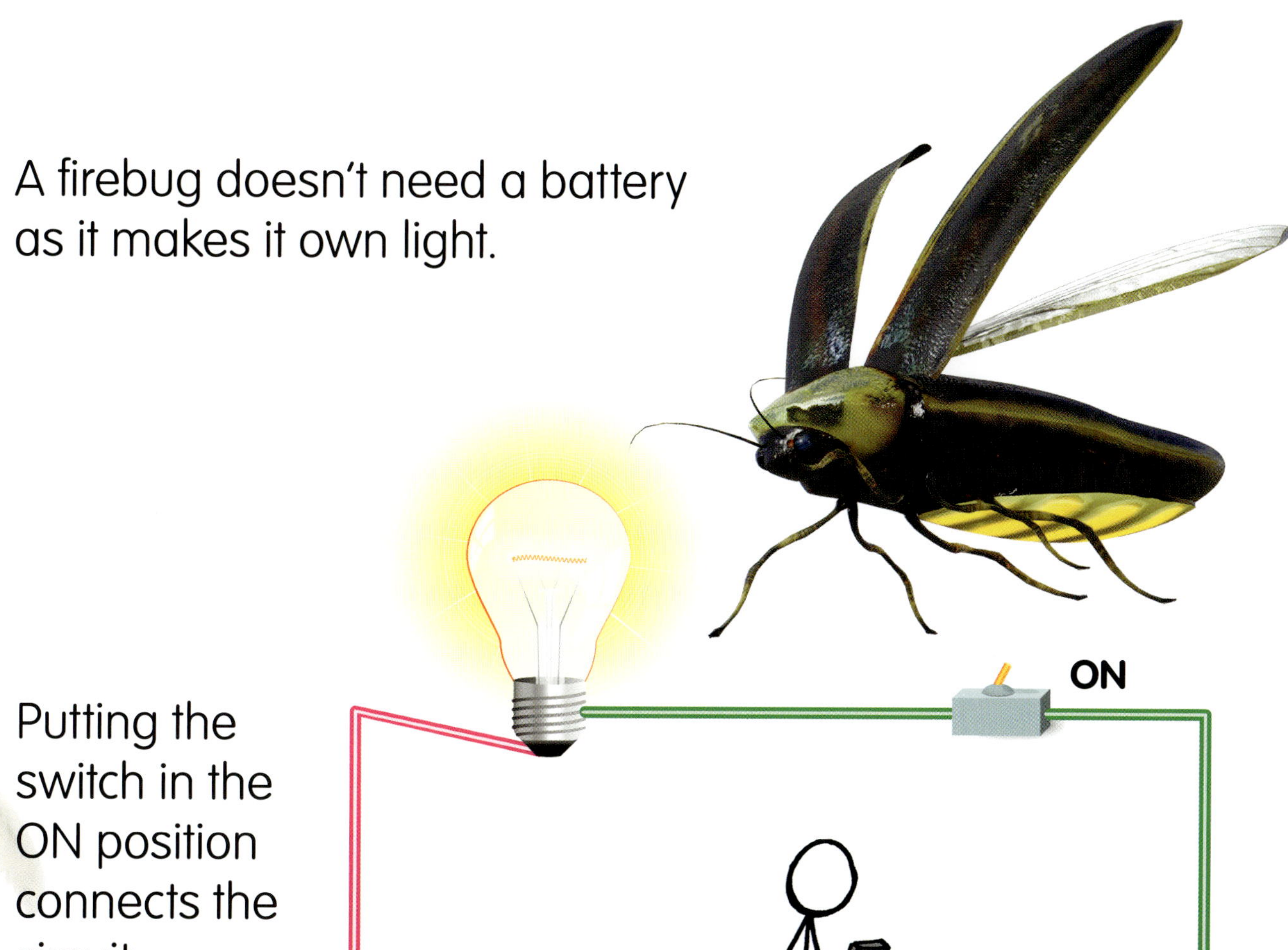

Putting the switch in the ON position connects the circuit.

Stickmen's Challenge Now it's your turn . . .

ON

OFF

Switch ON

When the switch is turned OFF, the light bulb is not lit. What happens when the switch is turned ON?

OFF

CONDUCTORS

Electricity will only flow through some materials. These materials are called electrical **conductors**.

Materials such as glass, plastic, wood, and stone are bad conductors because electricity does not flow through them.

Metals such as copper and steel are good conductors because electricity flows through them.

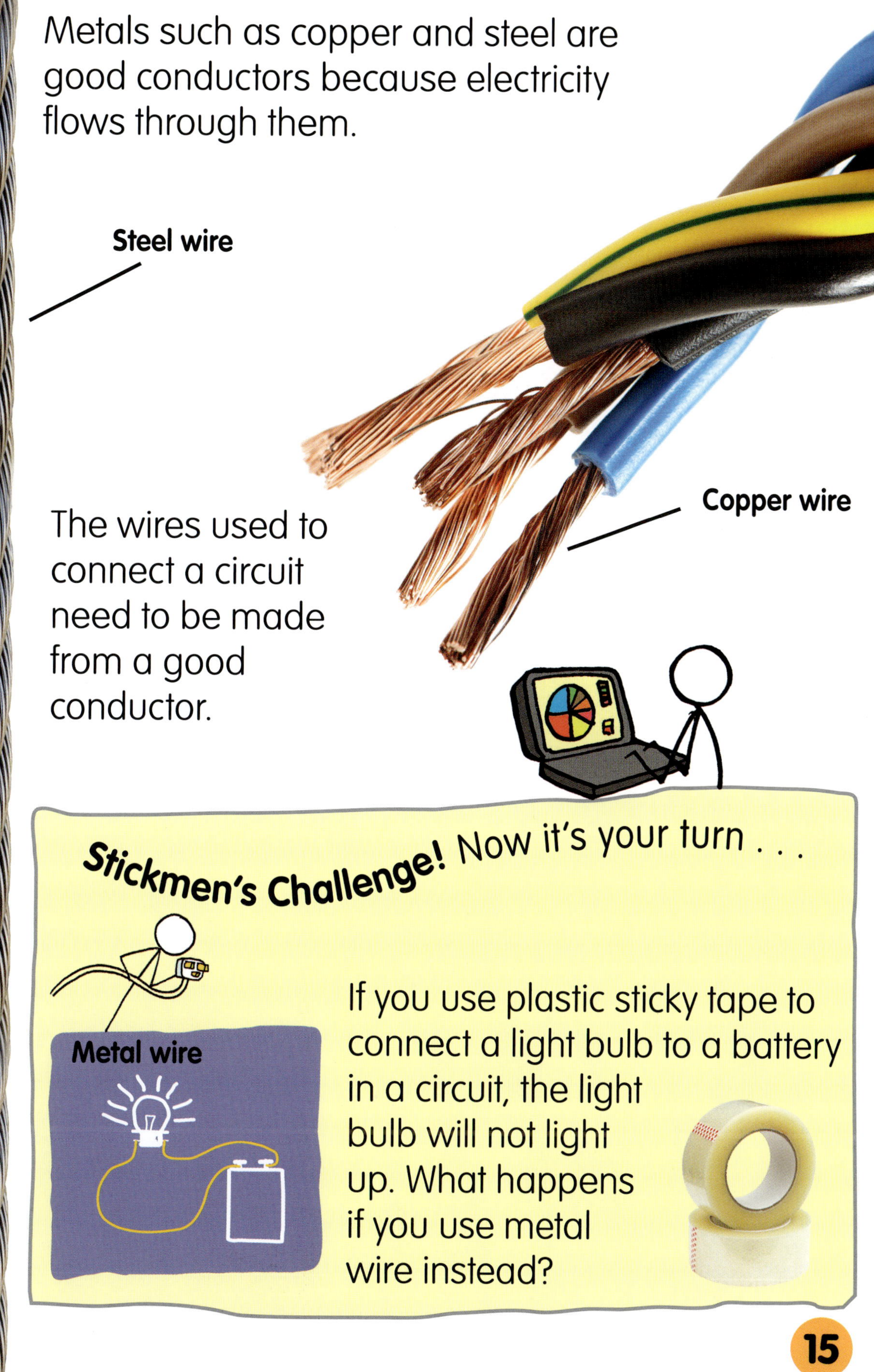

The wires used to connect a circuit need to be made from a good conductor.

Stickmen's Challenge! Now it's your turn . . .

If you use plastic sticky tape to connect a light bulb to a battery in a circuit, the light bulb will not light up. What happens if you use metal wire instead?

INSULATORS

A material that electricity cannot flow through is called an electrical **insulator**.

Air is also a good insulator. Electricity cannot flow across the gap between the two wires.

Wood, stone, glass, and plastic are good insulators.

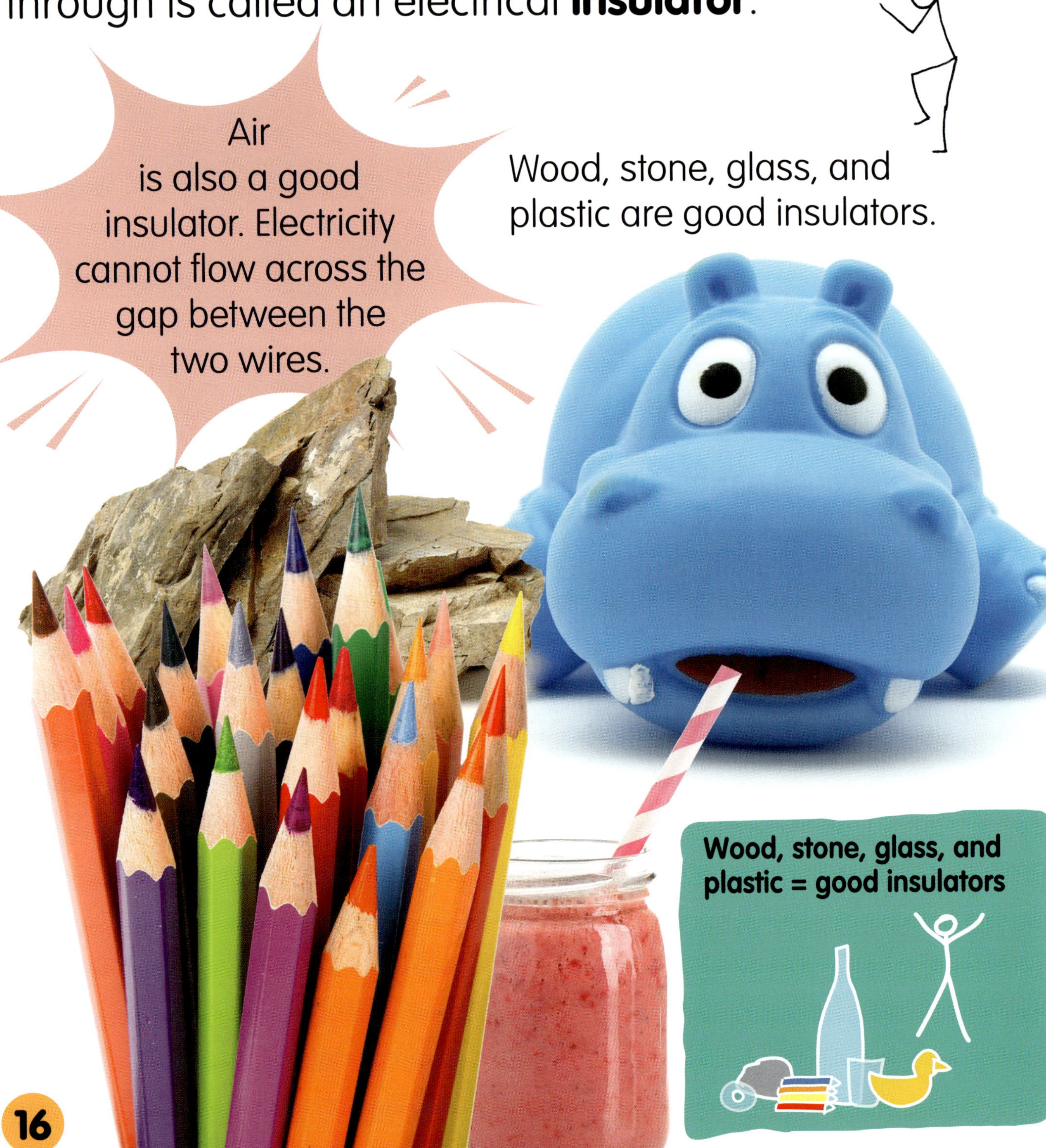

Electrical wire is often covered with plastic as an insulator.

The plastic insulation keeps the electricity in the wire and stops it flowing into other conductors.

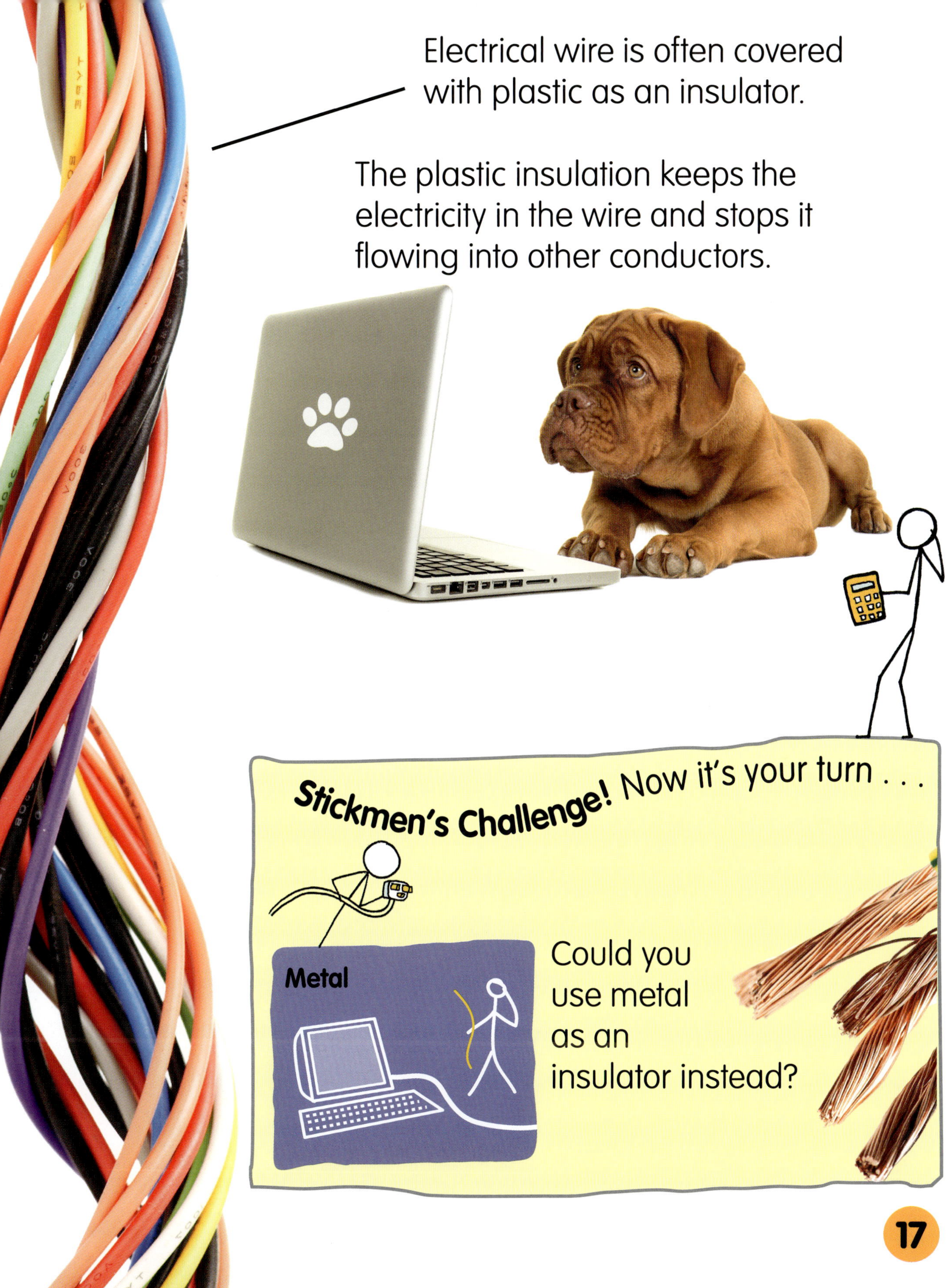

Stickmen's Challenge! Now it's your turn . . .

Could you use metal as an insulator instead?

GRID POWER

Homes, offices, and factories use **grid power**. It is much more powerful than the electricity in batteries.

Grid power is supplied to homes and offices through thick wires called **power lines.**

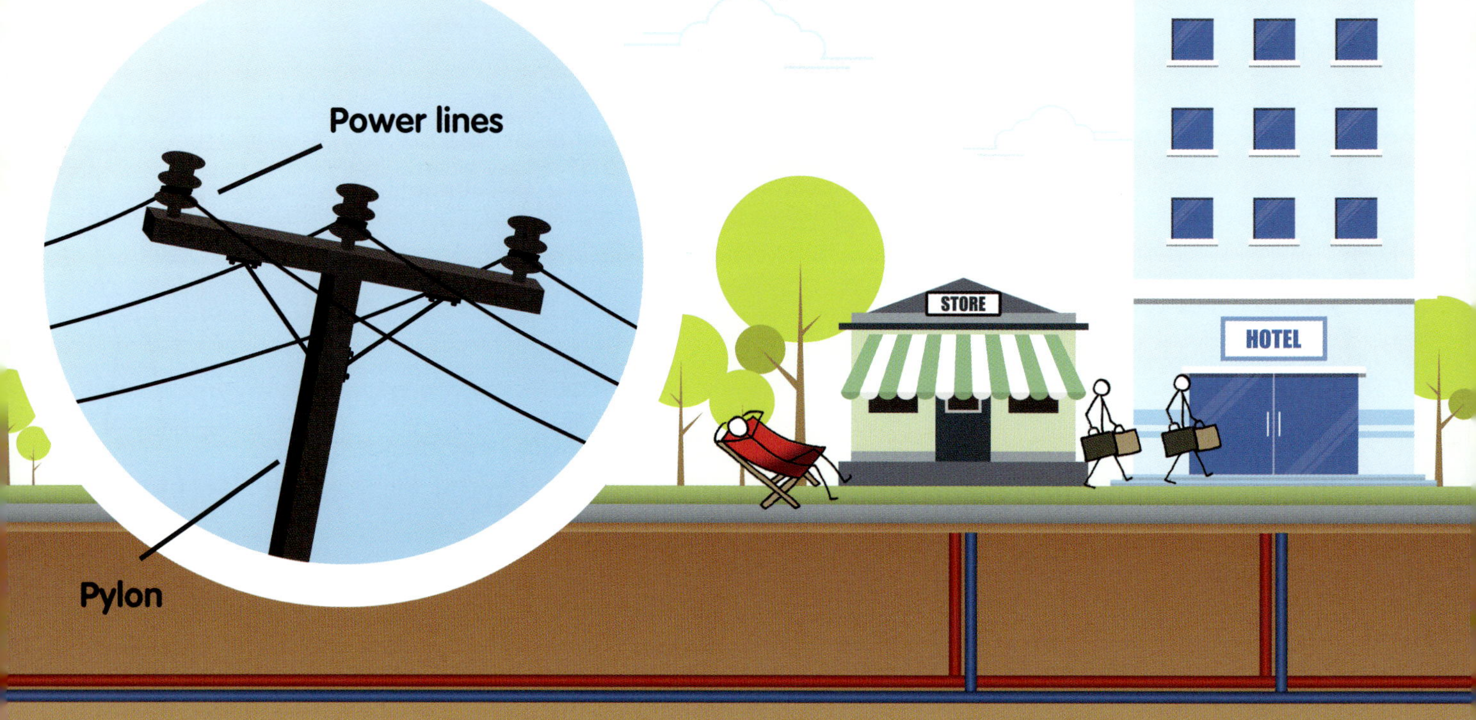

Power lines

Pylon

STORE

HOTEL

Power lines can be buried underground. Sometimes they are held up by tall towers called **pylons**.

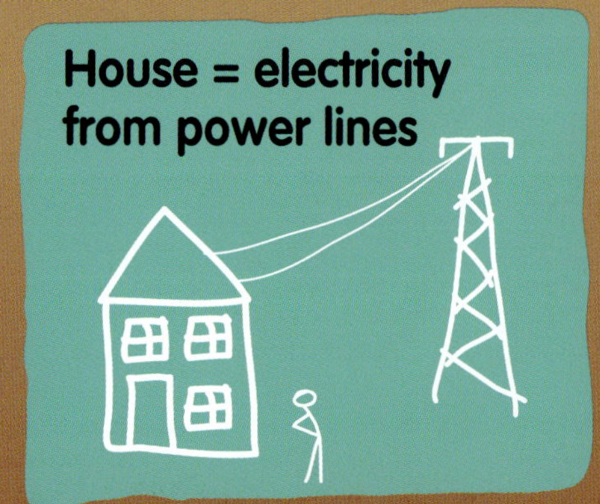

In offices and homes, electricity flows from the power lines through wires to electrical sockets. Machines that need a lot of electricity can be plugged into these **sockets.**

Electrical socket

DANGER
The electricity from grid power is strong enough to kill you. Do NOT poke your fingers or anything else into an electrical socket.

Small batteries can make a flashlight work, but do you think they can make a big fridge work?

ANSWERS

Page 5

A flashlight uses electricity to make light.

Light from a flashlight = electricity

Page 7

When there is no electricity going through the wire in the light bulb, it does not get hot and glow—so there is no light.

Light bulb + no electricity = no light

Page 9

Flashlight B will not work. Batteries will only work if they are put in the right way:

+ to + – to –

Battery wrong way around = flashlight B not working

Page 11

The circuit is not connected properly, so the light bulb does not light up.

Circuit not connected = light bulb does not light up

Page 13

When the switch is ON, it connects the circuit. This allows electricity to flow, which lights the light bulb.

Switch ON = electricity

Page 15

If you use metal wire, the light bulb will light up because metal wire is a good conductor of electricity.

Metal wire = good conductor

Page 17

Metal cannot be used as an insulator because it is a conductor!

Metal = bad insulator

Page 19

Small batteries are not strong enough to make a fridge work. A fridge uses grid power from an electrical socket.

Fridge = electricity from a socket

GLOSSARY

batteries objects that store small amounts of electricity

circuit the nonstop pathway, or route, that electricity flows along

conductors materials that electricity can flow through

electricity a kind of energy that powers machines and is used to make heat and light

insulator any material that electricity cannot flow through

light a kind of energy that we see with our eyes

light bulb a hollow glass object containing a thin wire that gives off light when electricity flows through it

grid power the electricity used by homes, offices, factories, and stores

metals hard, strong, shiny substances, such as steel and copper. Metals are good electrical conductors

power lines thick wires that deliver electricity to homes, offices, factories and shops

pylons tall, metal towers that are used to hold up power lines

sockets small boxes where appliances and machines, such as fridges or computers, can be plugged into the grid power supply

switch an object that is used to connect or disconnect an electrical circuit. Switches are used to turn electrical machines on and off.

INDEX

First published in 2020 by Hungry Tomato Ltd
F1, Old Bakery Studios, Blewetts Wharf, Malpas Road, Ruro, Cornwall, TR1 1QH, UK

ISBN 978 1 913077 525

Manufactured in the USA

www.hungrytomato.com

A CIP catalog record for this book is available from the British Library.

Picture credits
Shutterstock: 1: Javier Brosch. 2-3: Phongsagon Sangkasri. 4-5: WilleeCole Photography, ProStockStudio, wk1003mike. 6-7: prince_apple, Stock2You, Dimedrol68_shadow, Ermolaev Alexander. 8-9: Yeti studio, Oleg Kozlov, GraphicsRF, Kuttelvaserova Stuchelova. 12-13: Designua, Valentyna Chukhlyebova14-15: Suriyub, TheFarAwayKingdom, Rattachon Angmanee, ChartsTable789., MAKSYM SUKHENKO, Fedorov Oleksiy, TADDEU. 16-17: igorad1, Africa Studi, Vorobyeva. J IANG HONGYAN, Nata-Lia, MirasWonderland. 18-19: studio23, Pretty Vectors, jakkrit pimpru, By jakkrit pimpru.

Every effort has been made to trace the copyright holders, and we apologise in advance for any unintentional omissions. We would be pleased to insert the appropriate acknowledgements in any subsequent edition of this publication.